TELLING LIES

A SAM MASON K-9 DOG MYSTERY - BOOK 1

L A DOBBS

Chapters:

Falling.

This is my attempt
at describing the pains
that I feel inside of me,
descriptions of moments
that have left me breathless,
and my first attempts at
learning to breathe again.

On the bad days,
I close my wide eyes
and tell myself,

*"someday, you
will only remember
days like this,"*

reminding myself that
the hurting will not be
an everlasting thing, that
it is just passing through,

that it is here on purpose,
and finding that purpose
is an adventure that will
change me forever,
all for the better.

 - here for a reason

It's hard to trust,
to try again, to let
a little light in when
you've been shown
so many times that
the light goes just as
quickly as it comes.

Sometimes,
I find myself caught
in thoughts, tangled
up and thinking,
"the world would be
a brighter place if we
all simply only said the
things that we mean."

That is not this world.
People lie. Good times fade.
The sun still sets on our
happiest of days.

But here's the beauty of it all:
this endless marathon of reasons
to never try again, they all
give someone, something, the
chance to come into your life
and prove all of that wrong,
the opportunity to show you
that despite all that can go wrong,
something so damn beautiful
can still go right.

      - golden flakes of hope

I don't like people who
cannot keep their word.
It was engrained in me when
I was 8 years old and all of
the cars outside of school
were taking off one by one:
as more and more of them left,
I swear, I could feel time halting
as I slowly came to the realization
that I'd have to walk back inside
and deal with the dismal look on
the office ladies' faces as I say,
"they didn't show up again."

- a quiet ride home

I've been away lately.
See, I've been *seen* here,
but I've been closed-off
behind these open eyes.
My body lies here,
unscathed and untouched,
but an important part of me
isn't where it used to be.

I couldn't tell you where
my soul has wandered off to;
perhaps, it's napping in
another dimension, right
next to the guardian angel
that used to keep me
safe from this.

I think it's grown sick of me,
the way my pessimistic thoughts
climb on top of one another
to form skyscrapers of
unnecessary suffering.

But if there's one thing
that I rest assured of,
it's that I will not be
this person forever.

I promise,
I will not be
this person forever.

> *- where I've been*

Here's what they don't
tell us about love growing up:
the person you love the most, the
one who makes you the happiest,
is the one who holds the power
to also make you the saddest
you have ever been.

This fear, this standing at a cliff's edge,
is what keeps people, millions of them,
from ever finding something they
truly deserve: happiness.

- the fear of falling

My fear is that
you'll show up too late:
you'll come walking into
my life years from now,
and all I can tell you is,
"it's too late, soulmate;
I've given up on love."

- *find me soon*

You were the light
that came unexpectedly,
when I was convinced
I'd never see another
ray of sunshine
ever again.

You were that thing,
that one special thing,
that turned everything
upside-down, and made
a hopeless soul question,

*"maybe there is more
to this life of mine than
feeling miserable."*

And even though we
slowly fell apart, you
built a structure deep
inside of me that is still
standing today:

the idea that maybe it's
okay to let some people in.

- the start of something

You give an excuse.
I question it. You get angry.

*"That's not the reaction of
someone who loves you."*
I think to myself.

*"Love bears no anger;
loyalty doesn't stab the
recipient in the heart."*
My thoughts say.

I just smile and laugh,
telling you, *"babe, it's just
a joke. I'm not that crazy."*

This is just another time
I've suppressed how I feel
to keep us safe.

    - safety in submission

A small amount of air
leaves this room every time
you do something that seems
a little bit off, an act that makes
me think twice about trust
and your worthiness of it.
And though I'm not gasping,
this room is getting a little bit
too stuffy for my liking.

   - open a window and jump

Don't get too deep on me.
I'm not a fan of falling quickly.
I will run. I will run. I will run.

I know how this goes:
the feelings leave the atmosphere,
stranding us on a dead planet,
just as quickly as we fell here.

We'll be alone, far from home,
stranded in this relationship,
and we will feel nothing when
we look into each other's eyes.

So don't tell me you love me
when you've only seen the fire
of our beginning – not until I've
given you a million boring reasons.

Don't tell me you love me
when you've yet to see the war
that rages inside of me between
my angels and my demons.

Do not whisper a word of love
until you fully understand me.
I will run. I will run. I will run.

- too much too soon

I feel guilty when I do
the things we used to
with somebody new.

But for the sake of my
soul and sanity, I'm
letting that guilt go.

I can't give up on
walks in the park just
because that's where
we spent our Sundays.

I shouldn't feel bad
for eating your favorite
kind of ice cream when
I'm out starting over.

I can't abandon love
just because that's where
you abandoned me.

You don't deserve
that kind of control over
my life and happiness.

   - I'm setting myself free

I apologize for staying
when I knew I felt nothing.

- I should have left

It's hard to keep my
mind very far from you.

It tugs us together like my
lungs tug in the air around me,
as if thoughts of you are as
necessary as breath.

I tell myself often of just
how wrong for me you are.
This does nothing; it never
makes me want you any less.

Maybe my soul just hasn't
accepted the truth just yet,
or maybe it simply knows
something that I don't.

- in love and lost

I'm constantly at war with myself.
One half of me says that I should stop
thinking so much, that I deserve a break.
The other half tells me that if stop going,
even for just a minute, everything that I
have spent my entire life building will
fall apart right in front of me.

- as I sit and say nothing

We were the
most beautiful thing
I had ever known,
but this life I lead
isn't conducive of
beautiful things.

   - no home for beauty

I used to have
a space inside of me
for someone like you.
I filled it up with
the idea that
everyone's
the same.

- *seven billion*

I listened to a song recently; it
tugged politely at my heart strings.

It wasn't from words being sung;
it had no words, just a piano and
a cello swaying back and forth,
slow dancing in unison.

I could feel it. I could feel the love
the musicians had for each other,
and for a moment, I got jealous,
but then I realized:

Within the notes being played
was a message they left hidden
in plain sight, and when I unfolded
the melody and read what it said,
tears began to roll down my cheeks.

"If you feel this piece of music,
the love between the two of us,
you have once been loved,
and if you have once been loved,
you have truly been alive."

- a second to forget

I've been
heartbroken
since the first time
my mother told me,
"tie your own shoes.
I wont be here forever."

    - only human

I love you to death,
but I am so tired of
wishing you were here,
wishing my arms could
hold you the way I've been
holding onto these pillows,
wishing I didn't have to
wait a few minutes to get
a response to a question,
wishing my lips were
pressing against yours
instead of smashing down
into each other, quieting
me completely because
it's hard for me to talk
when my soul is hurting.

- far, far away

What hurts the most
about the pain in your eyes
is that happiness used to be
overflowing from where
tears now roll.

- where'd you go, my love?

If this is love, truly,
deeply, undeniably love,
why do I find myself
looking for a way out?

Why am I answering
your phone calls less?
I used to beg time to move
forward faster, so I could
hear from you sooner.

Can't you hear it in my
voice, the sound of me
falling out of love?

Don't you feel it in my
touch, a cold ash where
firestorms once raged?

I can't be the only one
noticing a difference.

Look at me
how you used to,
not the way
my parents did
before they split
the world
in half.

 - *stay together*

Have we run our course
or simply run off course?
Is there anything left here
that's worth being felt?
Tell me you're still happy.
Please, stop the bleeding
and tell me you still
want me to stay.

- still forever

I was born
with an emptiness,
a hole in my soul:
this void, I see now,
has always been
yours to fill.

- *come closer*

I never told you this,
but I am in love with you,
and I could fill the oceans
of this and other worlds
with the tears I have cried
over watching you
fall in love with
other people.

   - *friends forever*

I like to think of
love as an ocean:
with the further you
sink into it, the more
sadness is pressured
out of you. It's a kind
of drowning, but one
where only pain cannot
take breaths as you learn
to breathe under water.

  - *aquatic aorta*

When things
are falling apart,
remember this:
it was required
of stars to explode
for you to be here.

- this is an explosion

Soulmates don't
leave each other.

I don't want to be
remembered differently:
I want to live a life
so magnificent,
as-it-happened
is the only way
to remember it.

- strive for this

I still reminisce on us,
and I must confess:
you're just as beautiful
in retrospect.

You're as kind as ever.
You still make me smile
when I remember all of the
ways you made me laugh.

But that's the thing.
I'm not laughing at them
anymore; I'm just smiling.

The edges are dulling,
and the memories don't
quite cut so very deeply
anymore.

This thought gives me
one of my greatest fears:

that someday, I'll
forget you, us, everything
we had, entirely, and I wont
even be able to remember the
first thing I fell in love with –
the color of your eyes.

    - don't let me forget

It's hard just to
stand next to you,
to know that all of
the questions that have
haunted me for years
are just out of reach,
separated from me
only by your inability
to tell the truth.

- no honesty

Sometimes,
I still imagine us
finding each other
again later in life,
when the timing
is finally right.

- lifetimes later

I'm not afraid of falling out of love
as much as I am of growing out of it.
Because, I've seen what a few years can
do to a person, let alone two separate
human beings.

So maybe, when we're deciding who we
should invest our limited time into, we
should take into account how their heart
has changed over the years, and how we
think they might love us a few years down
the road.

I think true love is not only fitting into
someone else's heart and life today, but
also fitting into them both for every
tomorrow that is to come.

  - why we didn't work

I wont last like this
forever, pretending
your lips still give me
butterflies, that your
smile is still the reason
why I'm smiling.

 - *things changed*

I don't feel
human tonight.
I feel like body parts,
just a whole bunch of
things that don't really
add up to a human.

- incomplete

You and I will always feel
like an incomplete sentence,
like we were writing words
on a page, but the pen ran out
of ink before we had the chance
to pour the rest of our
beating hearts out.

- so much left to say

You didn't come home
like you always did; my
heart raced before it broke.

You didn't pick up
like you usually did; my
heart raced before it broke.

Your car was parked
outside of a small town bar;
my heart raced before it broke.

And there you were, all
wrapped up in someone else's
arms, an adulterous smile
as the ribbon on this
unwanted gift.

We locked eyes,
and the terror-pity
cocktail in yours
told me everything:

you weren't in love
with this stranger,
just no longer
in love with me.

My heart raced,
and then it broke.

- one drunken autumn

My heart
still pounds
in my chest
when you
come close,
as if it is reaching
out for yours in
the only way
that it
knows how.

   - 160 BPM

My head stays
in the clouds.
My thoughts fall
downward like rain.
And in this ink
is the downpour
of a mind that
gave up on reality
years ago.

- *clouded*

It was always
strange, bewildering,
as if we were
both speaking in
broken languages
that neither of us
could fully
understand.

We could not
communicate,
speak our minds
or hearts, and
that was what
destroyed us
in the end.

- *communication*

We don't have to let
things end like this.
It could still be forever.

We can still patch up
this life raft we used to
sail off into the sunset
and sail into it again.

Just like we used to,
we can hold hands and
live the dreams that
all kids are taught to
believe are possible.

Maybe, if we learn to
be forgiving enough,
we could even let all of
these mistakes go and
fall for each other
all over again.

- patchwork

Someday,
when the light
hits just right,
you will see it,
you will see just
how much you lost
when you took me
for granted.

- when the light hits

I just want to
feel understood.

I want someone
to look at me dead
in my tired eyes
and tell me,

"I understand you"

without ever even
saying a word, as we
continue on with our
lives in completely
different directions.

   - familiar strangers

I couldn't find
the words back then,
but if I were a poet
all those years ago,
and I had lost you in
the same exact way,
I would have jotted
down in my notes,

*"I lost all reason
to be myself the
day you left me
because of who
I am."*

   - years ago

I've lived my
worst nightmares,
and I've made it out
on the other side
of them still alive:
I am living proof
that nightmares
do end.

  - *the waking up*
    is beautiful

Healing.

I'm still hurt.
The difference is,
it's not getting worse.
I'm healing, getting better.
Someday, I will make it out
of the way I feel alive.

You've changed your mind
so many times since I have
known you, I don't feel like
I even know you anymore.

How many of your heartbeats
did you allow me to hear, my ears
pressed against your chest, after
it was no longer beating for me?

Did you stop telling me "*I love you*"
when you started saying it to
somebody else? Or did you just
start saying it twice as much?

I have questions, and you have
all of the answers, but, by the looks
of it, I fell for somebody who can
neither swallow the truth nor
spit it out.

So this is me, giving up on not only
all of the feelings I still have for you,
but on all of the questions I know you
don't have the spine to answer.

I'm letting the past fall away,
and I'm starting all over again.
You are nothing more than
yesterday's sadness.

- yesterday's sadness

I felt a lack of sincerity
every time you touched me,
but I already loved you,
so I stayed anyway.

I'd get sick to my stomach
when I wouldn't hear from you,
but I already loved you,
so I stayed anyway.

I'd give you my time,
and you'd take my breath,
and you'd just sit there
looking unimpressed.

The thing was,
I already loved you,
and you were after a chase
that lasted a little longer.

But to this very day,
even though it broke me,
I thank my lucky stars
that I fell hard and fast.

We might still be together
if I had held back a little longer,
and lord knows how miserable
a person like you would make me.

- lucky to lose you

I think of you,
and the day stands still,
as if time had legs.

And I'm overcome
with this brilliant sinking,
this downward push.

I won't let myself forget
for too long; forgetting means
giving up, and I can't do that
to myself again.

So even though I'm afraid
to love you, to put myself out there
and trust you with my heart,
I must hold on.

I'm taking off my running shoes,
settling down and settling in,
giving someone my all again.

And I'm not saying
what we have is forever;
I'm just saying that it
sure as hell could be.

- barefoot (no more running away)

I've grown close to
the fear of attachment:
letting someone feel like
you will always be there
creates just enough room
for them to take you
for granted.

- your company matters

I may hurt you someday.
I've done such terrible things.
My hands and my heart are
equally calloused, so I wouldn't
blame you if you let the fear of
me breaking your heart hang
over you like a raincloud
that just wont go away.

- expecting rain

My father asked me,
*"would you sacrifice
yourself to save her?"*

"In a heartbeat." I said.

He then asked,
"would she do the same?"

"I don't think so." I replied.

*"Well, knowing this,
would you still do it?"*
he questioned.

"In a heartbeat." I spoke again.

He smiled, placed his
hand upon my shoulder,
and declared softly,

"This is love."

   - 2am in the backyard

I stopped feeling
your absence so deeply.

I gave up on double
texting you like I was
giving up smoking.

I once thought,
"my god, did I just smile
at someone who isn't you?
Is this flirting?"

It felt like I had cheated
on my own heart, but that
wasn't the case at all.

I see now that it was
something else:

I was falling out of love
with the idea of making
you and I work again.

- catching up to you

If you ask someone,
"are you feeling okay?"
the silence after the question
will tell you everything.

So count the seconds,
because you never know
what kind of pain is
hiding behind a smile.

You never know,
if you were to just stop
and try harder to get
someone to open up,

if you were to show them
that someone cares more
than they think anyone
ever possibly could,

then maybe, just maybe,
you could be the one who
kept them from becoming
someone who did something
they could never undo.

- a single step further

You're far too good to me:
your heart has always felt
out of my league, as if it

deserves someone better to love,
someone softer, kinder, capable
of more and higher levels of love,

someone with a shorter distance
between their skin and their heartbeat, someone who isn't so guarded
and quick to assume the worst,

someone who can take jokes
without thinking you might
actually mean them,

someone who will answer all
of your phone calls and come over
right away when you need them,

someone with a little less pride
within their heart and a little bit more
understanding in there instead.

- mermaid meets monster

I dreamt of you
again last night.
You kissed my lips,
and I woke up feeling
just as I had
all those
years ago.

   - *homesick*

I'm tired of thinking
about you this much:
tonight, I just want
sleep.

You do it even though
you know it breaks my heart;
you do it over and over
and over and over again:
you give me hope,
knowing so very well
I have no chance at all of
ever having your heart.

- giving me hope

I don't know much of life lately.
I'm really only certain of two things:
I love you, and I don't know
what to do about it.

- everything I know

It's strange how
in the blink of an eye
feelings just fall over
and stop breathing.

One wrong move,
one little act that
shows you haven't
been completely honest,

and suddenly,
I will never feel
the same for you
again.

I just can't bet my heart;
I can't place it in the hands
of someone who likes
to keep them in
their pockets.

This is why I run.
I see something in
someone early on that
I know will hurt me later.

    - predicting the future

Sometimes,
I feel out of place
in my own body.

And sometimes,
on the worst days,
I find myself
thinking,

*"Maybe I'd be
happier elsewhere."*

- in another life

I'll shed tears tonight,
but someday, I swear,
I'll have no tears left
to mourn us with.

All of my hope will be
placed in something else.

All of my thoughts will
orbit around new worlds.

All of this heartache will
be reshaped and recycled
into something that's both
beautiful and useful.

I'll cry only happy tears,
and, who knows, maybe
I'll even look back and smile
every once in a while.

- let the healing begin

It's the thinking
that breaks my heart
over and over again,
but it's in remembering
"love can happen twice"
that restores it
every single time.

- happening(s)

Life-changing.
You, my god,
you are so damn
life-changing.

And I'll
never be the same
because of how you
came into my life and
happened to me.

You just came
out of nowhere and
true love, all at once,
happily happened.

- I'm smiling

I'm in my head a lot,
not because I was born
to be an introvert, but
because the worlds
I build in my head
more closely resemble
how I always thought
this world would be.

- the day I left

I am not the angel you
have made me out to be:
in my light, there is darkness,
so much darkness, and I
just don't know what you
even see in me, or how
you're even seeing it.

- I feel pitch black

I woke up from
a nightmare last night
and breathed a sigh
of relief: I dreamt
I was my old
self again.

- *backwards in time*

Would it make
you feel better if
I shrank my world
down to the size
of yours?

Does my success
and happiness take
away from yours?

Does the thickness of
my castle walls make
you feel insecure
about yours?

Tell me, why would
you allow my happiness
to deprive you of
your own?

- to those I've outgrown

I often miss you
when I feel alone:
perhaps, it's just me
forgetting how big
the world is.

I have loved you for a lifetime.
We just never found the right time.
I swear, someday, this wait
will come to and end.

- we are forever waiting to happen

Consider this:
something perfectly fit
will take the place of what
has just slipped through
your fingers. And maybe,
just maybe, it's not very
far away from you. Perhaps,
it's only one day away from
changing your life
forever.

   - *making sense of things*

I left, but I didn't move on.
And it's been so long now,
but after all of this time,
I still ache to my very core
to tell you how these houses
have never felt like homes
since we've been apart,
how having you in my heart
but not in my arms
is so soul-crushingly
not enough.

- please, come back home

What you felt, it was something,
but it surely wasn't love. Because,
love and loyalty go hand in hand,
and I couldn't count on five hands
the number of times you broke
my heart in secrecy.

- five hands and counting

If you ever break my heart,
all I ask is that you don't
do it behind my back.

- tell me the truth

I had an outline for my life
before I met you: make
some money, find somebody
I can die with, and close my
eyes until time shoots us
both in the head.

   - *thanks for ruining my plans;*
     now let's go on an adventure

I'm so sorry to say this,
and it might mess up your day,
but you can't love someone
and not be loyal, so don't go
crawling back to them with
a mouth full of I-love-you's
and apologies.

  - *true love doesn't sleep around*

It was the little things,
in the end, that tore us
apart the most.

I'm willing to bet this world,
its moon, and every single star
that's plastered up above it,
on the idea that all soulmates
eventually come together,
even if it's only
for a moment.

- *moment of a lifetime*

Seven billion humans,
and I'm supposed to believe
that my soulmate is someone
born in the same city as me?
That they grew up right
down the road?

- faraway lover

I hope this happiness
isn't temporary.
I hope this is truly
the forever we
think it is.

I don't want to be
blindsided by another
clipping of my wings
just as I become okay
with flying again.

   - birds of a feather

If this is not love,
do not act like it is.

- give me honesty

Have you ever made
eye contact with a stranger
and felt your souls connect?
Perhaps, you were both
soulmates in a past life.

- no words exchanged

"I'm pretty sure
that pretty words
and soft lips will
be the end of me."

I wrote this the day we met.

"I'm pretty sure
that pretty words
from soft lips will
be the end of us."

I write this as you're falling
in love with someone else.

- while I sit at home

You've changed, and I'm still
not sure how to feel about that.
I've changed as well, and I guess
you're not very sure how to feel
about that either.

I think we both planted seeds
in our hearts, and they both grew
into different kinds of flowers.

I love you one way, and you love
me another, and maybe if things
were a little bit different,
that would be okay.

Our hearts, perhaps, just blossomed
into incompatible lovers.

This isn't what we want in the end,
but don't you ever go thinking
that this garden isn't beautiful.

And no matter how much
this has to hurt in the end,
the most heart-warming truth
is still there for us to see:

we helped each other grow.

I can't keep breaking. I can't keep
shattering myself over someone who
feels nothing for me. I can't keep losing
sleep. I can't keep running the water in
my bathroom just so nobody can hear
me crying late at night.

I can't keep wasting all of my thoughts
on fantasies of you coming and knocking
on my door and screaming through it of
how wrong and sorry you finally feel.

I can't keep my hopes up this high;
at heights like these, the risk of not
surviving is too much for me to take.

I can't spend the rest of my life
wishing I meant more to you.

This is my word, a final declaration,
I'm giving up on you. I'm finally letting
the idea of you and I go.

- I'm moving on

Perhaps, from time to time,
all we truly need is someone's
skin pressed up against our own,
their hands running through our
hair, and a few kisses against
our necks.

Because there's not much like
being around so many people
but never feeling like anyone
truly understands you, like they
don't feel the same longing inside
of their souls that you do.

- *lonely humans together*

In these dark days,
I turn my eyes skyward.
I look to the cloudy,
gray sky and tell it,

*"I get you. I get why you
feel like falling apart."*

And as the rain falls so
caressingly on my face,
I feel a little less alone in
all of this pain I'm facing.

I feel like, if nothing else,
at least I'm not falling apart
all by myself this time.

I have the winter sky to
look down at me and care
while I mourn all I have lost,
all I have not become, and
all I will never be.

- I surrender

"*Baby, you wont love me*
less tomorrow, will you?"
She asks shyly.

"*What kind of a question is that?*"
He returns gently.

She smiles half-heartedly,
"*A question someone who's been*
left behind before would ask."

- *afraid to ask*

I woke up,
rolled over,
and started
crying.

I can't believe
we're falling
apart.

But a part of me
understands that,
someday,

all of this pain
will make complete
and perfect sense.

  - *awaiting the day*

I was 16 and happy
when you first told me
that I was incomplete.

I went from feeling whole
to feeling holes in myself.

And I tried, god, did I try,
to fill them with the things
you said I needed.

It took me years to understand
that there was never truly
anything wrong with me.

There were simply gaps in your
own happiness, and you used me --
you used my innocence against me,

to mold me into who you wanted
to spend the rest of your life with.

You were miserable, so you
made me feel miserable too.

- 1632

There are hurricanes
in my bedroom tonight,
violent storms raging in
a place deep within me.

I awaken to thunder,
rainwater fills the room.

Forgiveness is some
kind of beautiful anarchy,
a necessary tearing
apart of oneself.

These hurricane force winds
are breaking down all of the
anger, hurt, guilt, and bitterness
that I have carried around for
what feels like forever.

This destruction in me will
be what finally makes the space
in my heart and soul for love,
positivity, and happiness.

- I'm ready to change

Letting Things Go.

More love. Less pain.
This is me letting things go.

I once read that pain
can be written out of us,
so I took a piece of paper
and wrote your name on it
until every inch was filled.

I quickly learned that healing
is more than just thinking
and talking about the pain.

It's more than taking the time
to acknowledge it: healing is
about learning to look at that
little piece of paper without
wanting to burn it to ashes.

So I took all of my matches
and tossed them in the trash.
I sat down with what was tearing
me apart on the inside and had
some conversations with myself
about why I can't let this go.

And that was the day
that truly changed everything,
the beginning of me finally
letting things go.

- daybreak

My neighbors planted a couple of
trees in their front yard the other day,
and I could not help but feel inspired.

I thought to myself,
"I hope I outgrow this dusty, old neighborhood."

My heart was suddenly flooded with hope.
"I don't want to be around to watch them grow."
I thought out loud before I finished,

*"I want to come back ten years from now,
place my palms against those trees, and thank
them for inspiring me to chase my dreams."*

And since that day, I've kept my
bedroom window a little bit cracked,
just so that I can see those twin trees
becoming everything they were
destined to become.

    - two trees and three dreams

I gave myself some time.
I'm done crying over you.
I'm done letting my weakness
be the source of your strength.
I'm done feeling this way.
I'm done losing sleep over you.
I'm done waking up early
from nightmares of us.
I'm giving up on everything
I used to want with you,
and, today, I'm opening
myself up to love again.

- open, again

I wanted something real.
You gave me something
that looked a lot like it,
and I accepted that
as good enough.

- my mistake

And now that years have passed,
it's time to begin forgiving myself
for the damage I caused with
the ways I coped with loss.

I never meant to break any hearts,
so it's time to stop breaking my own.

- heaven sent closure

I don't like falling.
Just like the sun,
I too want to set,
to slowly settle in,
to gently cease to be
shattered and miserable,
and softly rise again
together and happy.

- *soulsets at sunset*

If I could push a button that'd make
me love you a little less, I wouldn't.
This pain, this wishing you were here,
this loving you in spite of everything,
it reminds me that I am human. It
shows me day in and day out that
my heart is not over, that I am *still*
capable of bizarre amounts of love.

- *this lake has become an ocean*

I have black holes in my soul
where stars used to be, forever
reminding me that, sometimes,
beautiful things go out with
a big and beautiful bang.

  - *when a love vast enough*
  doesn't fizzle out of existence,
  it explodes

In late nights,
all by myself,
in the same bedroom
we used to love in,
I got over you.

Unlike you,
I didn't use
other people to
make myself
feel better.

The opposite sex
didn't cure my
heartache; no,
I did that all
on my own.

- *other people*

I used to be angry.
I can't be that anymore.

I used to be cold hearted.
I won't be so ever again.

I used to laugh at love.
I want to laugh because
I'm in love instead.

I used to think that my
yesterdays would always
be better than my tomorrows.
I don't care for such ways
of thinking anymore.

I've been hurt, and yet
I'm happier today than
I've ever been before, even
more so than before my
heart was ever broken.

I'm growing.
I'm forgiving.
I'm moving on.
I'm loving who
I'm becoming.

I'm on a collision course
with true happiness.

Love floats away sometimes,
but here's the best part about it:
sometimes, the reason why is
because the universe is just
making room for what you
truly deserve.

- *moving out, moving on*

I feel you coming the same way
my bones feel storms approaching.
My soul senses you, and I am so
ready to finally meet you after
all of these years apart.

- dear happiness

I hate relationships.
I hate trying to trust someone
when every atom in my body
tells me that trust is deadly.
I hate telling my story to
people who probably wont
last very long in my life.
I hate listening to theirs and
filling my head with things
I'll have no use for when
we eventually fall apart.
I hate doing this again
and again and again.

Despite all of that,
I still want to be proven wrong.
I still want to tell my story.
I still want to listen to theirs.
I still want to try again
and again and again.

   - I **still** want love

Things start to weigh on your heart, you know?
As years go by and people hurt you, your heart
becomes heavier, and you become far less willing
to take chances on people. You could've risked it
with this person in the past, but your heart is far
too heavy now, and you are sick of seeing people
become exactly who they say they aren't. It begins
to feel like one more heartache is all it will take
to make you give up on love completely.
Here's the secret: it's just a test; don't give up.

- the sinking heart

You say things,
and I retaliate:
this is not love.

- starting to see

I hope, someday,
you'll be lying right
next to me, your head
resting on my shoulder as
I write stories for the world
about how, sometimes,
it all works out in the end.

 - *I've found my muse*

You traded a star
for a nightlight, just
because it was dark out
for a little while.

And while my light
would have returned,
it never will now, not
after how everything
had to happen.

I've accepted this,
the fact that my light
was meant for someone
other than you.

- trading down

Since we last spoke,
I've grown a little older,
a little braver – a little
bit closer to who you
always said I could be:
myself.

- a little closer

And the next time
you saw me in public,
I was unrecognizable –
not in the way I looked,
but in the way
I carried myself.

- better attitude

I spent years believing
you couldn't quit because
you didn't love me enough.

I spent years hoping that
one day I'd wake up and have
the childhood I never had.

I spent years hoping and
praying and crying and it
never did a thing.

And now, I'm much older,
and my soul just hurts, and
I wish you'd for once just

be more than the person
who gave me life.

- years and years

I've always felt separate from
this world around me, these
people I'm supposed to be
getting to know.

It's odd: I couldn't tell
you my neighbors' names,
but I could tell you that the
husband beats the wife
at least twice a week.

My point is,
speaking to people isn't
always how you get
to know someone.

This is why I
separate myself
and just listen.

       - flies & walls

I still care.
I still care so very deeply,
but at some point,
you just have to close
your wide and tired eyes,
take the deepest of breaths,
and politely tell yourself,
"I still care, but I'm done being
tired and miserable. It's time
that I let some things go."

   - for my own sake

You were never afraid
of the destruction I was
capable of: I told you my
heart was a wrecking ball,
and that loving me was like
pulling the ball further back,
allowing it energy to destroy,
and you just walked up to me,
kissed my cheek, and said,

*"If this loving of you is what
destroys me in the end, I think,
that's an alright way to go out."*

- the gift of benevolence

I will still have
a happy ending,
even if we don't.

I'm throwing a
welcome home party
with my mind, heart,
and soul, and you're
invited. You are so
welcome here.

- *come over, happiness*

There's no greater
loneliness than waiting
for someone to love you
in return, hoping that
someday they will open
their heart and soul to you
the same way you have
opened yours to them.

But love isn't something
we should wait to happen;
true love is something that
just arrives and feels right,
like it belongs there
safely in your chest.

And you just can't
convince someone to feel
something they aren't
capable of feeling.

You can't force love
into someone else's chest.
You have to let them go
and find the person you
are truly meant to be with.

   - hearts are stubborn things

If there's love
in your heart,
speak of it.

If there's pain
where love once was,
tell the world.

If you're scared,
tell your story like
a secret confession to
someone you trust.

If you're proud,
wear your story like
a battle scar across
your face.

Someone will listen.

- advice to writers

I crave the
kind of feelings
that come from
falling in love with
someone beautiful
who, just like you,
wears their soul
on their sleeve.

- a pair of open books

Now that some
time has passed,
I can look back and
see things a little bit
more clearly.

What is the clearest
thing to see of them all
is this: in love with you
is a place I don't belong.

To find my happiness,
I have to go somewhere else,
look inside of myself and
fill the voids with my
own love, rather than
someone else's.

I see this now.
I am enough. I am enough.
I am worthy of my own love.
I don't need someone else
to feel like I am complete.

- some clarity

I just laugh at what
used to make me cry.
This has set me free.

- wind in my wings

Be with someone
who loves you harder
on the days you can't
love yourself at all.

- there for you

It has taken me years
to finally see the truth
that has been right in
front of me all along.

The truth is this:
let go of the people who
have let go of you.

They probably want you
to let them go, anyway.

- for you and for them

I saw my soul in a dream last night.
It was much prettier and kinder
than I always thought it to be.

We didn't have much time.
"I know why you're here."
I said softly.

Stardust was floating off my
soul in every direction as it said,
"You're giving up on me again."

It paused; I waited:
the silence cut so deep.
It grabbed both of my hands,
 "You can't keep doing this to me."

"Stop being so kind." I said angrily.
*"It's kindness that's gotten me here
in the first place."* I finished.

My soul never once broke character.
It brushed my hair with its glowing fingers,
just like my mother used to when I was
a little kid, telling me so sweetly,

"It's not your kindness that's gotten you hurt.
It's those who have given up on their kindness
that have broken your heart. Don't become them.
*Whatever you do, **just don't give up on me**."*

I woke up the next day a different person.

- with stardust in my hair

The sun will rise tomorrow,
and with it, I will remember
you a little bit less – the pain
of our yesterdays together
will be a little less present.

- fading slowly

Really, I'm just
trying to be happy
in a world that seems
to want my heart
forever broken.

I'm just trying to find
some inner peace and
a few reasons to get
myself motivated to
wake up each morning.

And I'm getting there.
I'm finding those reasons.
I'm finding that peace.
I'm healing my heart.

All I ask for is patience
as I learn who it is I am
meant to become.

- soul searching

Looking back now,
the day I lost you
was actually the day
I started blooming.

- thank you

Where I'm at is
a place so beautiful,
I struggle to pair my
heart with words.

Maybe if I knew
a few more languages,
read the dictionary
a little more often,

I could describe
my heart with
the same ferocity
in which I feel
the things I feel.

   - where I'm at

I woke up from a sleep one morning.
Again, I didn't dream.

I just sat there as I stared at the ceiling,
thinking no thoughts, feeling no feelings.

They say it's better to feel nothing
than to have your heart torn in half.

Well, I have felt both, and I would
much rather have pain in my heart
than an emptiness I don't even
know how to fill.

At least with heartache,
you can search for stitches.

With numbness, you're searching
for something you don't have that
everyone else seems to have been
born with: something, god, just,
anything worth living for.

That morning was the
last morning I'd ever feel
that way again.

This was the day I met you.

- and everything changed

Happy Again

Happiness and love can happen twice.
I am living, breathing proof.

Look into a mirror.
Stare at yourself, point out
all of the things you find pretty.

Be only kind to yourself today.
Please, be only kind to yourself.

Place every negative opinion you
have about your bone structure,
skin, heart, soul, and mind all into
your soft and loving hands, make
the tightest fists you can,
and squeeze them.

Let this friction, this love of yourself,
burn them to ash, and then watch them
drift off with the wind when you
open your hands again.

This is you opening up to yourself,
graduating, blossoming, into someone
much softer and kinder than you
ever were before.

You are your own constant reminder
that you *must* continue breathing,
that you *need* to keep taking breaths
and only speak love to yourself,
even when it hurts like hell.

- spring for the soul

I've learned you.
In late nights, I've read your
soul in volumes, listened to your
stories and touched your scars as
you told me how you got them.

You've opened up for me unlike
you have with anyone else before.

Those are the good days,
but not all days are bright.

Life gets complicated, and it's easy to
forget that there's still a sun up above us
from beneath these clouded skies.

But knowing what you've been through
makes it easy for me to believe that
everything will somehow be
alright for you in the end.

I know your past. I know the sadnesses
you have outlived. I know the secrets
you rarely confess. And that is why
I love seeing you happy.

- a sparkling in your eyes

If the lights go out,
I will light a candle.
There will be no kind
of darkness here –
not in this home,
not in this family,
not in this love.

- there will be only light

It is a new day;
I am a different person,
born again, taken away
from the weight I carried.
Today, I will retake my
very first step and
very first breath.

   - somo
   (starting over; moving on)

Let's hold hands on the moon
and watch the world end together.

- the perfect date

I swing from the branches
of my family tree, kissing
each and every piece of fruit
politely on the cheek, a gentle
little reminder that even
though we don't speak,
I still love you all.

- *heritage*

I like to believe that all angels
who give up on their wings
eventually find their way
back to them in the end.

- I hope you're healing

It's okay;
you'll only
be miserable
for a while.

If things
had worked out,
you'd instead
be miserable
forever.

  - *the bright side*

My idea of love changed the
day we met. Suddenly, it didn't
always have to slowly blossom;
no, sometimes, it shows up and
overtakes you all at once.

In an instant, butterflies are born
and any fog that obscures your view
of the future melts away. You see,
sometimes, love not only gives you
so many reasons to smile; it also
changes the way you think.

And if that's not beautiful,
I simply don't know what is.

You raise my spirits like curtains;
the light leaks in all at once.

And as the darkness melts away,
I'm coming to find that my heart
is beginning to feel warm again.

I'm loving now that I feel loved.
I'm trusting now that I feel trusted.
I'm warmer to people now that I
feel like sunlight.

I feel alive again.
I feel like I've started all over,
but what's different is, this time,
I'm pointed in the right direction.

And there's a lot to say about
no longer feeling lost inside.

- compass for the soul

If we ever part ways,
I hope it's in old age,
and I hope we're
holding hands
as we go.

- *truly forever*

I've always had parts hidden.
I've always dressed up my personality
in clothes that didn't fit me, trying to look
like a person someone might want.

I wore robes that made my soul feel small,
masks that hid my true feelings. All of this,
it was before I learned to love myself.

This was before forgiveness came and
made it feel okay to be myself, as if who
I am underneath it all is someone somebody
might actually want to meet, someone
they'll want to love.

And since I've stopped hiding myself,
I can't stop smiling, and I can't stop
telling myself that life is beautiful
and worth every bit of pain that
comes along with it.

- who I am today

They tell us not to find
happiness in other people,
but, my god, do you make
me so incredibly happy.

I want to break every rule,
jump the fences most people
fall in love from and do
everything our own way.

- lawless lovers

I was about ten,
learning about life as
I went along with it.

My nights after school
were spent skipping
my homework and
gluing myself to the
corded phone that
hung on the wall.

The happiest I felt was
when we had already run
completely out of words
so many hours ago, but we
were far too obsessed to
hang up the phone.

Listening to your soft
and loving exhales as you
politely listened to mine
was utter bliss for us,
two kids who simply
could never quite get
enough of one another.

I want that again,
the childhood innocence,
the mysterious bliss feeling,
to love someone so very deeply
without even knowing
what love even is.

    - *"you hang up first"*

You don't put me down
for being myself. You fill
the room with laughter every
time I say something silly,
when others before you
would fill the room with
awkward silence.

I tell you,
"I'm afraid of getting hurt again."
You just smile and tell me,
"You deserve happiness,
so stop being so afraid of it
and let me make you happy."

So this is me, letting you
make me happy, opening up
after being closed off from love
for what feels like lifetimes.

I'm risking everything and
letting you get close to me.

Thank you for opening me up.
Thank you for changing everything.

- perfect match

When I'm gone,
I hope the universe
takes sweet care of you,
sees to it that the pain of life
never truly outweighs
the joy of it.

- *my wish for you*

Promise me you won't
give up on all you want.

- I want you to have it all

Fight for me.
Every day, just fight
to make this work.

If we aren't destined
for each other, it'll hurt
and wont work out, but
I'm just so tired of living
my life afraid of risking
everything.

I'm tired of holding my
heart in my own hands; I
want to see what it looks like
resting safely against the palms
of someone else.

I want to know that it isn't
too heavy for someone else
to carry. So stay. And wage
wars for me like I will for you.

If we get hurt, we'll get hurt
badly, but at least we'll know
we gave this everything that
we have to give.

- I want to be all-in with you

You never let
me hate myself. I say
something I don't like
about myself, and you
tell me twenty things
you find beautiful.

That's twenty to one,
and I always fair no chance
against those odds.

Someday, I swear, I'll accept
all of myself, and I'll have you
to thank for bringing to light this
new way of living, this perspective
on myself that I never
gave a chance.

I adore your soul.
I want the same for you,
and if I must, I'll spend the
rest of my life convincing you
that you're beautiful, too.

- soft hands

I can't promise you
that tomorrow will come,
but I can promise you
that if it does, I will
still be yours.

 - *forever yours*

Over the years,
I have grown, changed,
altered the shape of my
mind, heart, and soul.

And now,
I have stretch marks
on all three of these from
the growing I have done.

I'm not ashamed of
the scars of growth I
carry around and wear
proudly on my being.

I've been hurt, damn
nearly destroyed, but I
refused to let all of that
pain be for nothing.

I can stand here today,
proud of and in love
with who I have become,
because I once
was broken.

- *useful damage*

I drink coffee because of my mother.
She would leave for work, and I would
know she was gone if there was half a pot
of black coffee cooling off on the counter.

I'd ask for a little glass some mornings,
and she would tell me, "you're too young;
you don't need coffee until you're older."

I didn't understand it back then.
The thing was, I already *felt* old: life
had forced me to grow up quickly.

We were poor, and I was young,
and I was exposed to some evils that
a child should never lay their eyes on.

But that black coffee cooling off on the counter,
it was a literal representation of just how hard
my mother was working to take care of her
children - to take us somewhere better.

I wanted to be like that; I wanted to
work as hard as my mother did, to give
everything I have to someone I love.

So every morning, coffee touches my lips,
and suddenly I'm 5 years old and watching
my mother leave the house before 6am,
coffee mug in hand, ready to give her all
for what she loves the most.

- coffee and generations

You shouldn't have to carry
the weight of two happinesses,
just yours and yours alone.

- *let go, tired soul*

Love can happen again.
Happiness can come back.
Peace after pain is possible.
In darker days, you must take
sweet and gentle care of yourself,
put your spirit first and learn how
to put some of the things you
 have been carrying around down.
A slow beginning is all it takes,
one small act of kindness after
another, to yourself, is what
adds up to a lifetime of feeling
like you're loved.

- *inward acts of kindness*

These days aren't so dark;
at least, they aren't as dark
as they used to be, and I've
learned not to ask for very
much more than *just enough*
when it comes to healing.

Just enough courage
to take the very first step
away from somebody.

Just enough peace
to fall asleep with at least
half a smile at night.

Just enough hope
to feel like tomorrow might
actually be worth visiting.

Just enough rainwater
to wipe my soul clean –
rid me of the fingerprints
that make me feel
untouchable.

I ask for the bare minimum
until I'm strong enough to
demand more of myself.

A slow and gentle start
is the safest way to heal
a tired and broken soul.

   - *you are not ruined*

The things we have let go of,
we have let go of for a reason.

So on the bad nights, when
we toss and turn and loneliness
is leading our thoughts back
to those very things again,

we have to hold those reasons
so very tightly against our chests,
so very gently in our arms.

Hold those reasons instead
of holding onto the pain.

And as for the pain,
let it go – let all of it go.
This is how you move you.
This is how you start over.
This is how you let things go.
This is how you fight to be
happy again.

                - *a better way*

After years
of torturing myself
with the idea that I
could never let certain
things go, I gave up on
that idea, and, suddenly,
I could feel my fingers
beginning to slip.

And in time, there
will come a day where I
will feel all of my sorrows
brushing gently against
my fingertips as I watch
them finally fall away.

I will be free.
I will be home again.
I will be happy.

   - *a pleasant goodbye*

A letter,

Thank you so very much for making it this far, not only in my book, but in your life. Take a moment to thank yourself for being so strong and kind that you have allowed yourself to make it to this very day without giving up completely. These things in themselves, our lives and good health, are accomplishments worth celebrating.

I'm honored to have shared a piece of myself with you. I've written down parts of my heart, mind, body, and soul into these pages. I've spoken of some things that I have never said out loud. I've said some words here that might not be taken in the best way by some of the people they were written about. But isn't that what art is all about? Celebrating, bringing to light in one way or another, the fact that none of us are perfect? The fact that, in the end, we're all just humans?

At the end of the day, I just hope that in reading this book of mine, you have found some source of light, or strength, or hope, or happiness, or anything positive, really. I hope that by investing your time into my work and I, you have come out of this book, just like me, a better person because of it. Writing this book has changed my life in some very dramatic ways.

I'll talk about that in the next one.

                                        With love,
                                        Faraway

Made in the USA
San Bernardino, CA
22 August 2018